BASEBALL
— IN THE —
BARRIOS

BASEBALL
- IN THE -
BARRIOS

HENRY HORENSTEIN

Gulliver Books

Harcourt Brace & Company

SAN DIEGO   NEW YORK   LONDON

Baseball in the Barrios is dedicated to Dumbo Fernández
and all the great Venezuelan players who never had
a chance to play in the big leagues.

Requests for permission to make copies of any part of the work should be mailed to:
Permissions Department, Harcourt Brace & Company, 6277 Sea Harbor Drive,
Orlando, Florida 32887-6777.

The baseball cards on page 10 are courtesy of Line Up Co.
The photographs on page 11 are courtesy of The National Baseball Library & Archive,
Cooperstown, New York.
The map on pages 34 and 35 was rendered by Patti Isaacs, Parrot Graphics.

Gulliver Books is a registered trademark of Harcourt Brace & Company.

Library of Congress Cataloging-in-Publication Data
Horenstein, Henry.
Baseball in the barrios/Henry Horenstein.—1st ed.
p.   cm.
"Gulliver Books."
Summary: Hubaldo's life as a fifth grader in a barrio in Venezuela centers around his
love for his country's most popular sport, its teams, and its players.
ISBN 0-15-200499-8
ISBN 0-15-200504-8 (pbk.)
1. Baseball—Venezuela—Juvenile literature.
[1. Baseball—Venezuela. 2. Venezuela—Social life and customs.] I. Title.
GV863.41.A1H67   1997
796.357′0987—dc20   95-39779

Text set in Clearface
Display set in Windsor Bold
Designed by Kaelin Chappell

First edition
A B C D E F
A B C D E F (pbk.)

Printed in Singapore

At night as I fall asleep I imagine the sound of fans cheering: "Hubaldo! Hubaldo! Hubaldo!" There are two outs; the count is 1 and 2; and the score is tied 1–1. The pitch is tough—high, inside, and fast. But I don't back away. With one smooth stroke, I send the ball over the left field fence. I trot around the bases. My teammates greet me as I tag home plate. We win the game—and the national championship.

I'm called Hubaldo (oo-BAL-doh), but my full name is Hubaldo Antonio Romero Páez. Antonio is my middle name, just like Anthony in English. My father is Pedro Romero and my mother is Carmen Páez, so Romero and Páez are my family names. In Venezuela, where I live, we use both our parents' family names and our mother's goes last.

The most popular sport here is baseball—or *béisbol* in Spanish. My mom says baseball has been played in Venezuela almost as long as in the United States. That makes it an *all*-American sport—played in North *and* South America.

Like most of my friends, I'd rather play baseball than do almost anything else. Of course, I do have to go to school. I live in Caracas, the capital and largest city of Venezuela, and I'm in the fifth grade at Escuela Básica Carmen Maizo de Bello *(escuela básica* means elementary school). We start school every morning at seven o'clock and finish at three o'clock, which leaves plenty of time to play baseball in the afternoon and do my homework at night. At school we are graded with numbers ranging from 1 to 20. Ten is passing; 15 is pretty good. I average 16 to 17 points every term, so I'm a good student but no genius. My real talent is in baseball, and when I finish school I want to be a professional ballplayer. I know it's tough to make it, but I'm sure it's not impossible.

Venezuela is much smaller than the United States, but we do have two professional leagues: the Winter League and the Summer League. The best players by far are in the Winter League, which has eight teams from all over Venezuela. Some of the best teams are los Tigres de Aragua (the Aragua Tigers), las Águilas del Zulia (the Zulia Eagles), and my favorite team, los Leones de Caracas (the Caracas Lions).

The Winter League season begins in October, about the time of the World Series in the United States, and ends with play-offs in February. The winning team plays in the Caribbean Series against the best teams from Puerto Rico, Mexico, and the Dominican Republic.

Many of the best players from Venezuela spend summers in the United States and become major-league stars. My favorite player is the slugging first baseman Andrés Galarraga—we call him The Big Cat. In the winter he plays for the Leones, and in the summers he has played for the Montreal Expos, the St. Louis Cardinals, and the Colorado Rockies. I also like the swift-fielding shortstops Omar Vizquel and Ozzie Guillén. Vizquel plays for the Leones and the Cleveland Indians, and Guillén plays for los Tiburones de La Guaira (the La Guaira Sharks) and the Chicago White Sox.

Andrés Galarraga
Primera base

Omar Vízquel
Shortstop

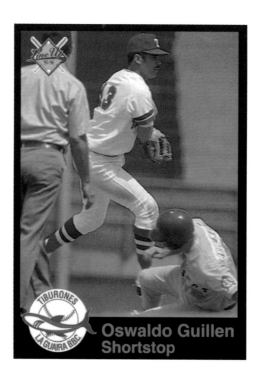

Oswaldo Guillen
Shortstop

Chico Carrasquel

Luis Aparicio

My dad's favorite players are from the 1950s and the 1960s—the great shortstops Alfonso "Chico" Carrasquel and Luis Aparicio. Carrasquel was a powerful hitter with the Leones. He played for the Chicago White Sox and the Cleveland Indians in the United States and was the first Latin player to make the major-league All-Star team. That made him a hero back home in Venezuela. Aparicio played for los Petroleros de Cabimas (the Cabimas Oilmen), then for the Chicago White Sox and the Boston Red Sox. He was a great fielder and is now a member of the Baseball Hall of Fame in Cooperstown, New York.

There are dozens of Latin American players in the major leagues these days, but very few made it before the 1950s. My mom says language differences and transportation were much more of a problem in those days, and Latin players felt more comfortable playing at home, with friends and family around. There was also a lot of prejudice against Latins, just like there was against black players.

To be a good ballplayer, you must start early, and in Venezuela there are many opportunities to play organized baseball, even at a very young age. When I was four years old, I started playing with the Semillitas, which means little seeds. The idea is that seeds will grow into big ballplayers. We won the city championship, and there was a picture of me with my friends Romni and Rodni and the rest of our teammates in *El Nacional,* one of the largest newspapers in Caracas.

Semillitas work out at least once a week. They run around the field to get in shape, then they take fielding and hitting practice. They even play formal games, though they need a lot of help from grown-ups. I remember my first hit. I was so surprised that I ran right to my mother instead of to first base.

In Venezuela each team has a godmother, or *madrina*. She watches the game and cheers for her team, bringing it good luck. The *madrina* is usually about the same age as the team she represents—even for the Semillitas.

As I got older I played with the Preparatories and the Preinfantils. Now I'm with the Infantils, which is the league for ten- and eleven-year-olds. We practice three times a week and play formal games once a week, usually on Friday nights.

My team is called los Trompos, which means tops—and we are. So far we're in first place, mostly because of Romni's excellent hitting—he leads the league in home runs—and Rodni's outstanding pitching. I play shortstop, like the great Carrasquel and Aparicio. I hit pretty well, but if I make it to the major leagues it'll be because I'm a good fielder and I'm fast. Very few ground balls get past me, and I try to steal a base whenever I can.

Our field seats about three hundred people. On game nights it's packed with the players' parents and families, and emotions run high. Fathers scream at the umpires when their sons are called out. Some mothers, like my mom, try to calm their husbands down, but many mothers scream louder than the fathers.

Baseball is played in all parts of Venezuela, from the Amazonas Territory in the south to the Andes Mountains in the west. Most famous ballplayers come from the cities, though, probably because most of the country's people live in urban areas. Almost four million people live in and around Caracas. Some city neighborhoods are called *urbanizaciónes,* and others are called barrios. I live in the San Andrés barrio.

My family is very close. My mother takes care of the kids while my father is at work. She comes to all my games, with my little sister, Marbelis. Marbelis likes to play ball, but she's not nearly as good as I am. I have two older brothers—Pedro Jr. and Victor—and they are also good ballplayers, but they don't get to play as much as they'd like because they both have jobs.

My father doesn't play baseball anymore, but he spends as much time as he can at games.
He rides me to team practice on his motorcycle, and at home he teaches me the fundamentals—
like how to turn the double play, how to steal second base, and how to slide around the tag.
These are the fine points of the game that often make the difference between winning and losing.
Dad and I also spend a lot of time talking about baseball and organizing my card collection.

Like most of my friends, I like to collect baseball cards, *barajitas de béisbol.* Maybe they'll be valuable someday, but for now I use them to play a game called *paredita* with Romni. We each put a card flat against a wall. Then we count to three out loud—*uno, dos, tres*— and let our cards fall to the ground. If my card falls on Romni's, I keep my card and take his. If Romni's card covers mine, he gets to keep both cards.

Venezuela is just north of the equator, and in Caracas, it's warm and sunny almost all year-round. During the summer it is often eighty or ninety degrees, and even most winter days are warmer than sixty degrees. This means we can play baseball all year long. My favorite time is from December to May, though. That's the dry season, and during those months we never get rained out.

If you take a walk through a typical barrio in Caracas almost any day, you'll see all kinds of baseball being played. We don't really need a field. Just about any place will do. We play a lot of informal or pickup games. We call them *caimanera*. Some kids play baseball on basketball courts or on the pavement, which can really hurt when you slide into a base.

Others play in the hills around Caracas; this kid is tossing a ball around on his lunch
break at the farm where he works. The old bus holds supplies and feed for his horse.

Of course, we have regulation fields, too. These are run by the government and used for league play. But there aren't nearly enough. Some fields are well kept, but others sometimes need a good mowing. I remember hitting a legitimate single *(sencillo)* to left field once and getting all the way around to third base before the fielder found the ball in the outfield grass and tossed it back to the infield.

Sometimes kids break into fields when they are closed. Usually they just want a place to play, but sometimes they cause damage. So the fields are closed off when they are not being used, and in some places broken soda bottles are placed on top of the walls to help keep trespassers out.

In league games we use normal bats and gloves. But you don't really need any special equipment to play baseball. You can use a crushed plastic oil can or a flattened shopping bag for home plate *(la goma)*. Planks of wood make great bats—or *bates*—although you have to watch out for splinters. Rolled-up socks, rags, crushed orange juice containers, or even wads of paper are good substitutes for baseballs *(pelotas)*. This kid's even hitting a cabbage with a stick. I don't think this *pelota* will travel very far—or last very long.

One of the most popular forms of baseball in Venezuela—and all of Latin America—is called *chapitas,* which means bottle caps. We collect bottle caps wherever we can—from grocery stores, off the road, even out of trash cans. Then the pitcher flips the caps one at a time to the batter, who uses a broomstick to try to hit them.

Chapitas are very difficult to hit. They are small and it's hard to follow their movement. It takes excellent concentration to make contact, and many people believe Latin ballplayers hit so well because they train their eyes playing *chapitas.*

Hard rubber balls *(peloticas de goma)* are also popular because they travel a long way and they're cheap—40 Bs, or bolívares. Bolívares are the main units of currency in Venezuela. One bolívar is worth a little more than half a cent in the United States, so forty bolívares is about twenty or twenty-five cents. Our currency is named for Simón Bolívar, our greatest national hero, who is known as *El Libertador,* the Liberator, and also as the George Washington of South America. At the beginning of the nineteenth century, he fought to free Venezuela and other South American countries from Spanish rule.

My friends and I practice a lot with tennis balls. They don't cost much and they don't break windows as easily as baseballs or *peloticas de goma*. Whenever we don't have a formal game, I meet Romni and Rodni and we go to the nearest playground and play ball. We laugh a lot, but we're pretty serious about it. Sometimes we play for hours. Then we sit around and talk about the next los Trompos game and our favorite professional players.

When I get home, I'm exhausted and ready for bed. Unfortunately, on most nights I haven't done my homework. I try to explain to my parents that I need my sleep for tomorrow's game, but they won't budge. They always say I need my studies more. "Even major leaguers need to read and write well," they say. I'm not sure about that, but I do my homework anyway.

Later, as I close my eyes to go to sleep, I imagine myself on second base. I look into the dugout and nod at Rodni. I see the legendary Chico Carrasquel standing next to him. The game is tied 1–1, and it's the bottom of the ninth inning. Romni is up and looks my way as he steps into the batter's box. The pitch comes in—fast, high, and inside. Romni goes with it and lines a single to right field. I'm off at the crack of the bat. I know it'll be a close play at home, so it's a good thing Dad has taught me how to slide around the tag. After all, if I beat the throw, we win the game—and the World Series.

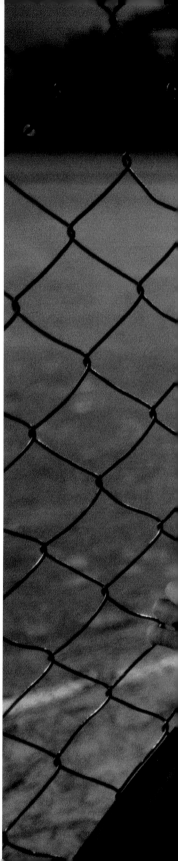

A Baseball Vocabulary

Many of the words used in Spanish to talk about baseball are the same or almost the same as in English. For example, umpire is umpire and manager is manager. Of course, many of the pronunciations are different. Here are some Spanish words that are important to know if you're a baseball player:

EQUIPMENT

Ball	Pelota (pay-LOW-ta)
Bat	Bate (BAH-tay)
Cap	Cachucha (ka-CHOO-cha)
Glove	Guante (GWAN-tay)
Helmet	Casco (KAS-ko)
Uniform	Uniforme (oo-nee-FOR-may)

THE FIELD

Dugout	Dogaut (DOH-gaut)
Home plate	La goma (la GO-ma)
First base	Primera base (pree-MAY-rah BAH-say)
Second base	Segunda base (say-GOON-da BAH-say)
Third base	Tercera base (tayr-SAYR-ah BAH-say)
Right field	Jardinero derecho (har-dee-NAY-ro de-REH-cho)
Center field	Jardinero central (har-dee-NAY-ro cen-TRAHL)
Left field	Jardinero izquierdo (har-dee-NAY-ro is-kee-YEHR-dough)
Stadium	Estadio (es-TAH-dee-o)

GAME

Fair ball	Fear ball (FER BOL)
Foul	Foul (FOWL)
Fly ball	Fly (FLY)
Single	Sencillo (sen-SEE-yo)
Double	Doble (DOUGH-blay)
Triple	Triple (TREE-play)
Home run	Jonrón (hon-RON)
	or Cuadrangular (kwa-dran-gu-LAR)
Bunt	Toque de bola (TOW-kay day BOW-la)
Double play	Doble matanza (DOUGH-blay mah-TAN-sa)

POSITIONS

Pitcher	Pitcher (PEE-cheyr)
Catcher	Cacher (KA-cheyr)
	or Receptor (ray-sep-TOR)
First baseman	Primera base (pree-MAY-ra BAH-say)
Second baseman	Segunda base (say-GOON-da BAH-say)
	or Camarero (ka-ma-RAY-ro)
Third baseman	Tercera base (tayr-SAYR-ah BAH-say)
	or Antesalista (AHN-tay-sa-LEE-stah)
Shortstop	Campo corto (KAM-po CORE-toe)
Outfielder	Jardinero (har-dee-NAY-ro)
Hitter	Bateador (bah-tay-ah-DOR)

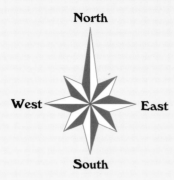

North

West   East

South

CARIBBEAN SEA

●Caracas

Venezuela

Guyana

Colombia

Brazil

North
America

*PACIFIC
OCEAN*

Acknowledgments

My warmest thanks to all my friends in Caracas for making this book happen. My hosts, Carlos Moreno and his wonderful family—Morelia, Carlos Jr., and Rolando—and the Harnists—Patrick, Mary, Cathy, Patricia, and Christine. Juan Morales and Ramón Fernández were great, as always. Thanks also to Graciano Ravelo, scout for the Kansas City Royals and director of the best baseball school in Venezuela; Roberto Avilán, Jesús Velásquez, and Richard Mejías, manager and coaches of Hubaldo's team; Mike Perez of the Line Up Company; and Dionisio Acosta, president of the Venezuelan Players' Association. Also to my talented and tireless translators, who generously doubled as photographic assistants—Cecilia Herrera and Beatriz Sampietro—and to Hubaldo's good friends and teammates—excellent ballplayers all, especially Romni Losada, Rodni Ramírez, and Harold Navarro. And, of course, many thanks to the Romero Páez family, who not only made the book possible, but made it great fun as well.

On the North American front, I want to thank Jonathan Landreth; Andreina Lauria; Megan Doyle for her assistance every step of the way; Andrea Raynor for her sharp editing eye; Kristi Worden for her early layout assistance; Kaelin Chappell for her design; and most of all, Anne Davies, for believing in the book and helping to shape it.